Mia's Family

BY ELLIOT RILEY

ILLUSTRATED BY
SRIMALIE BASSANI

Rourke
Educational Media
rourkeeducationalmedia.com

Before & After Reading Activities

Teaching Focus:

Concepts of Print: Have students find capital letters and punctuation in a sentence. Ask students to explain the purpose for using them in a sentence.

Before Reading:

Building Academic Vocabulary and Background Knowledge

Before reading a book, it is important to set the stage for your child or student by using pre-reading strategies. This will help them develop their vocabulary, increase their reading comprehension, and make connections across the curriculum.

1. Read the title and look at the cover. *Let's make predictions about what this book will be about.*
2. Take a picture walk by talking about the pictures/photographs in the book. Implant the vocabulary as you take the picture walk. Be sure to talk about the text features such as headings, the Table of Contents, glossary, bolded words, captions, charts/diagrams, or Index.
3. Have students read the first page of text with you then have students read the remaining text.
4. Strategy Talk – use to assist students while reading.
   - Get your mouth ready
   - Look at the picture
   - Think…does it make sense
   - Think…does it look right
   - Think…does it sound right
   - Chunk it – by looking for a part you know
5. Read it again.

Content Area Vocabulary
Use glossary words in a sentence.

produce
shelter
twins
volunteers

After Reading:

Comprehension and Extension Activity

After reading the book, work on the following questions with your child or students in order to check their level of reading comprehension and content mastery.

1. *What is Mia's parents' surprise? (Summarize)*
2. *What does Mia's family like to do together? (Asking Questions)*
3. *How is Mia's family like yours? How is it different? (Text to self connection)*
4. *Who are the people in Mia's family? (Asking Questions)*

Extension Activity

Draw a picture of your family enjoying an activity together. Below the picture, complete this sentence:
My family likes to _____.

Table of Contents

Meet Mia

This is Mia.

These are Mia's moms.

Mia has two brothers. They are **twins!**

Helping Hands

Mia's family **volunteers** together.

Mia and her brothers put fresh **produce** in bags.

The food is given to other families that need it.

Furry Family

Mia's family also volunteers at an animal **shelter**.

They bring toys and treats.

Mia reads books to the dogs.

The twins play with the cats.

17

Mia's moms have a surprise.

Two new family members!

Mia loves her family.

Mia's family loves Mia.

Picture Glossary

 **produce** (PROH-doos): Fruits and vegetables grown for eating.

 **shelter** (SHEL-tur): A place where homeless animals are cared for.

 **twins** (twinz): Two children born at the same time to the same mother.

 **volunteers** (vah-luhn-teers): Doing a job to help others without pay.

Family Fun

Who are the people in your family?

Draw each person and write their name below their picture.

How is your family portrait like Mia's? How is it different?

About the Author

Elliot Riley is an author with a big family of her own in Tampa, Florida. She loves when everyone gets together to eat, laugh, and play games. Especially the eating part!

Meet The Author!
www.meetREMauthors.com

Library of Congress PCN Data

Mia's Family/ Elliot Riley
(All Kinds of Families)
ISBN 978-1-68342-315-7 (hard cover)
ISBN 978-1-68342-411-6 (soft cover)
ISBN 978-1-68342-481-9 (e-Book)
Library of Congress Control Number: 2017931164

Rourke Educational Media
Printed in the United States of America,
North Mankato, Minnesota

www.rourkeeducationalmedia.com

Author Illustration: Srimalie Bassani
Edited by: Keli Sipperley
Cover design and interior design by:
Kathy Walsh